THe Bad
Luck Day

To BTS—
"Starlight that shines brighter in the
darkest night."
—G. S.

Daisy Dreamer

The Bad Luck Day

By Holly Anna • Illustrated by Genevieve Santos

LITTLE SIMON

New York London Toronto Sydney New Delhi

LITTLE SIMON

An imprint of Simon & Schuster Children's Publishing Division

1230 Avenue of the Americas, New York, New York 10020

First Little Simon hardcover edition November 2019

Copyright © 2019 by Simon & Schuster, Inc.

Also available in a Little Simon paperback edition.

All rights reserved, including the right of reproduction in whole or in part in any form.

LITTLE SIMON is a registered trademark of Simon & Schuster, Inc., and associated colophon is a trademark of Simon & Schuster, Inc. For information about special discounts for bulk purchases, please contact Simon & Schuster Special Sales at 1-866-506-1949 or business@simonandschuster.com. The Simon & Schuster Speakers Bureau can bring authors to your live event. For more information or to book an event contact the Simon & Schuster Speakers Bureau at 1-866-248-3049 or visit our website at www.simonspeakers.com.

Designed by Laura Roode

Manufactured in the United States of America 1019 FFG

2 4 6 8 10 9 7 5 3 1

Library of Congress Cataloging-in-Publication Data

Names: Anna, Holly, author. | Santos, Genevieve, illustrator.

Title: The bad luck day / by Holly Anna ; illustrated by Genevieve Santos.

Description: First Little Simon paperback edition. | New York : Little Simon, 2019. | Series: Daisy dreamer ; #11 | Summary: "Every kid in the world has had a Bad Luck Day, but Daisy Dreamer's might be the unluckiest Bad Luck Day ever"—Provided by publisher.

Identifiers: LCCN 2019011406 | ISBN 9781534442641 (paperback) | ISBN 9781534442658 (hardcover) | ISBN 9781534442665 (eBook)

Subjects: | CYAC: Luck—Fiction. | Art—Fiction. | Schools—Fiction. | Imaginary playmates—Fiction. | Magic—Fiction. | BISAC: JUVENILE FICTION / Imagination & Play. | JUVENILE FICTION / Humorous Stories. | JUVENILE FICTION / Readers / Chapter Books.

Classification: LCC PZ7.1.A568 Bad 2019 | DDC [Fic]—dc23

LC record available at https://lccn.loc.gov/2019011406

CONTENTS

CHAPTER ONE

The Sticky Octopus

Boing!

Boing!

Boing!

I, Daisy Dreamer, am hopping around like a bouncy kangaroo. That is how I pull my leggings on for school. *Obviously.* I also like to stretch my waistband out like a kangaroo pouch. Then I let it go. *Thwack!*

As I hippity-hop, I spy a purple blob behind my nightstand. I reach down and grab it!

It's my super-sticky octopus wall walker! It's been missing *for ages*. I got it at a birthday party a long time ago. I squish it in my fist and it smooshes out the sides. Then I hurl it against the wall and watch it crawl to the floor. It looks totally alive!

I run over and grab it and throw it again. And again! Then something crazy, but not totally crazy for me, happens. A door in my wall opens, and my imaginary friend, Posey, pops out.

"Hi, Daisy!" he cheers.

Posey surprises me right in the middle of winding up to throw, and the wall walker slips out of my hand.

Ka-blammo! The squishy, sticky octopus flies into my desk calendar and knocks it onto the floor.

"Oh no, Daisy!" I shout. I always say "Oh no, Daisy" when I knock things over.

Posey laughs and runs over to grab my wall walker. I run after him and pick my calendar up off the floor.

Then I notice the date. "Uh-oh!
Today is FRIDAY THE THIRTEENTH!"

Posey wrinkles his furry forehead
and says, "So?"

I set the calendar back on my desk. "Don't you know that Friday the thirteenth is a very unlucky day?"

Posey stares at me blankly.

"What does 'unlucky' mean?" he asks.

I try not to roll my eyes. How could Posey not know the meaning of 'unlucky'? I give him some examples.

"Unlucky is when you pop a bubble and the bubble gum gets stuck in your hair, or when your ice cream falls off your cone and lands in the dirt."

He still looks confused, so I tell him unlucky is the *opposite* of lucky.
Posey shakes his head.

"I do *not* like the sound of unlucky," he says. "I'm going to stick with plain old lucky—just like this octopus *sticks* to the wall."

Posey chucks my wall walker as hard as he can. SMACK! It hits my full-length mirror . . . and my mirror *cracks!*

The Broken Mirror

"DAISY?!" my mom shouts from down-stairs. "Is everything okay up there?"

I look to Posey for help.

"Don't worry! Today is your lucky day!" he says. Then he runs over to the broken mirror and flings a fistful of imaginary friend dust at it.

Wa-la! The cracks vanish and the mirror is fixed.

"DAISY!" Mom calls again. "Please answer me!"

I sprint to my door and pull it open. "Everything's FINE!" I yell back.

I hear my mom walk to the bottom of the stairs.

"Okay!" she says. "Two minutes till we leave for school."

I dash back into my room and put my hair in pigtails. Then I shove my pencil case, math homework, and books into my backpack.

"Gotta go!" I tell Posey.

But Posey's not listening. He's all tangled up in my sticky octopus. It's stuck to his antlers and both of his hands. He tries to pull it off one hand and then the other. It just won't let go!

I help him get untangled.

"Guess what?" I say as I unhook a tentacle from his antler.

"What?" Posey says.

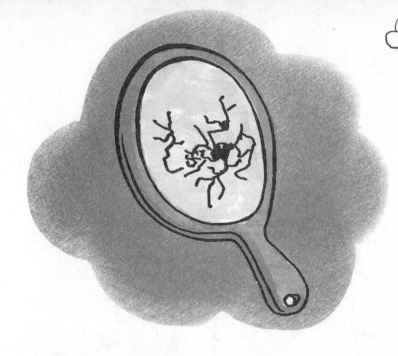

"People say that breaking a mirror gives you seven years of bad luck."

Posey shrugs. "But the mirror's not broken anymore, so it doesn't count."

I set what's left of my wall walker on my desk. "Well, I sure hope you're right."

Posey pats me on the back. "Is anything unlucky happening right now?"

I look around my room, and he's
right: Nothing unlucky is happening.

"See?" Posey says as he waves good-bye and disappears back into the World of Make-Believe. I start to head downstairs, but just to be safe, I hold on to the banister.

☆ Chapter Three ☆

A Black Cat

Jasmine and Lily meet me on the playground. They are both yawning.

"We got to school really early today!" Jasmine says.

"And we stayed super late yesterday!" Lily adds. They act sleepy, but I can tell they are so excited and I know why.

"Today is the art show!" I say.

Every year Weaverley Elementary holds an all-school art show. This year Jasmine and Lily volunteered to help set up the show.

"Are you coming?" Jasmine asks.

"Of *course* I'm coming!" I cheer. *"Obviously."*

We laugh and dance around in a circle. Then we race to class. For some reason, my backpack begins to feel lighter and lighter as we go.

I stop and look behind me.

"Oh my GOSH!" I cry. My yogurt container is splatted open on the ground. My apple is rolling away.

My friends turn around to see what's going on.

"Oh no, Daisy! Is that your math homework? It's blowing in the wind!" I see my math homework cartwheeling toward the swing sets. I chase after it. Then—*muckity-muck!*—my math book and social studies book fall into a mud puddle!

"Argh!" I wail.

Jasmine and Lily run to my side. Jasmine has my sandwich, and Lily's holding my bruised apple. They see my books lying in the mud.

"Whoa!" Jasmine exclaims. "How could anyone be *that* unlucky?"

I groan and take off after my math homework.

"WAIT!" Lily yells. I reluctantly stop and turn around. Lily's pointing at a black cat. "If that cat crosses your path, it could mean *more* bad luck!"

I look at the cat. Then I look at
my math homework, which is on the
other side of the cat. If I lose my math
homework, I'll have to do
it *all* over again! That
is totally *not* worth
it—so I cross the
black cat's path.
But it's no use.
A gust of wind lifts
my homework up in the
air. It swirls and lands on
the roof of my school. *Seriously?!*

I look back at the cat.

"*Mrr-o-o-w!*"

That must mean "Tough luck" in cat language. The cat curls up in the grass and glares after me.

What a BAD kitty! I think as I walk back with droopy shoulders. I can tell this is going to be a very *long* day.

☆ Chapter Four ☆

The Ladder

I pinch each of my dripping-wet books by a corner and carry them all the way to my classroom. Then I plop them on my group table. I couldn't help it. My pincher fingers were hurting me. *Obviously*. But now our table is all muddy and puddly.

Gabby Gaburp pushes my wet books away with a ruler.

Gabby is not my favorite person in the class. She sits across from me. Suddenly her hand flies up. Our teacher, Mr. Roberts, calls on her.

"Daisy Dreamer just made a complete *mess* on our table!" she complains. Then she turns and glares at me.

I pretend not to notice.

Mr. Roberts comes over to our table with a damp rag. First he wipes off my books. Then he sweeps the muddy water into the rag, but the rag doesn't do its job. Now the muddy water is all over *me!*

I shoot out of my seat like a Stomp Rocket. Gabby looks at me and bursts out laughing. Her meanie best friend, Carol Rattinger, joins in. Now the *whole* class is laughing at me. My face begins to feel hot and prickly.

"Oh, Daisy!" Mr. Roberts exclaims. "I am *so* sorry. Please feel free to go to the girls' room and clean up."

I grab the hall pass and run straight out the door. I can still hear kids laughing. *Whew,* am I glad to be away from all *that.*

As I walk down the hall I begin to think about my terrible luck today: *My lunch is ruined. My homework is on top of the school. My books fell in the mud. And my teacher accidentally wiped dirty water all over me!*

I'm so caught up in my thoughts that I don't notice the ladder set up in the hall, and I walk *right* under it. *Uh-oh.* Walking under a ladder is also bad luck. I freeze. *What's going to happen NOW?* I wonder. *Is the floor going to open up underneath me? Will I get sucked into an air vent?*

I slowly tilt back my head and look at the teacher, who's standing on the ladder. She just hung a banner for the art show. The teacher smiles at me, and then . . .

SNAP! The banner comes undone and falls down right on top of me. I just stand there in disbelief. Now I can hear the teacher's shoes climbing down the ladder. She pulls the banner off my head.

"Are you okay, honey?" she asks.

I give her a fake smile and say, "I'm fine."

But I am not fine. I have wet paint smudges on my face, arms, and shirt. I look like a complete *clown*. *Obviously*.

Then I sprint to the girls' room.

Mirror, Mirror

I push gently on the girls' room door and carefully check my surroundings. *What will happen NEXT?* I wonder. *Will a bat swoop down from the ceiling?* I tiptoe across the tiles. *Will the toilets start over-flowing?* I peer into each stall. I wonder which is worse, bats in my hair or leaky toilets.

This bathroom seems normal.

I hurry to the sink. First I wash the paint smudges off my face and arms. Then I rub the spots on my shirt with a damp paper towel. It doesn't all come off, but it looks much better. I check the mirror to make sure I haven't missed anything. But what I see makes me gasp.

"OH MY GOSH!" I yell, jumping back, like, two whole feet. It's Posey again. Only this time he's inside the mirror! "You scared the bajeebers out of me!"

Posey muffles a laugh with his hand.

"I'm sorry! I didn't mean to scare you," he says. "But I found something you dropped."

Then he reaches his arm right through the mirror and gives me my lost math homework! I grab it.

"*Wow*, Posey!" I cry. "You're the absolute *best*!"

We high-five through the mirror.

"No problem!" he says.

At times like this I'm sure happy to have my very own personal imaginary friend.

"I have to get back to class," I say, starting for the door. "But thanks again!"

"WAIT!" Posey calls out. "May I come with you?"

I turn around. Well, of course I would love to say yes, but the last time Posey came to my class, it was a *total* disaster.

So I say, "How about you join me at the art show after school instead?" Posey-in-the-Mirror gives me two thumbs up.

Then I skip all the way back to my classroom. My luck is changing for the better. *Obviously.*

Chapter Six

Imaginary Opposites

But I am wrong. So. Very. Wrong.

Before I get to my classroom, an imaginary door opens up right in the school hallway! And it's *Posey*. *Again*.

"Daisy, I'm glad I found you," he says in a very serious voice. "We need to *talk*."

I can feel my eyebrows squish together.

"But we *just* talked, like, fifteen seconds ago," I say, wondering what happened to the happy-go-lucky Posey I left in the bathroom.

Then Posey grabs me by the arm and yanks me away from my class-room door.

"OH NO!" he cries. "WE DID? This is just what I feared!"

I stare at him because I have no idea what he's talking about.

"What do you mean?" I ask, though I'm not sure I really want to know.

Posey grabs both my arms. "That wasn't *me* in the bathroom," he says.

I take a step back. I'm so confused. I *definitely* saw Posey in the bathroom, or at least, I thought I did.

"Listen," he says, "after you left for school, I went to the WOM library and researched the word 'unlucky.' I learned all about bad luck signs and superstitions. But I also learned that every imaginary friend has an *opposite*. Did you know that?"

I shake my head because no, I did not know that. To be honest, this whole imaginary friend thing is still pretty new to me.

"Well, I didn't know either," Posey says. "But I have an opposite who looks just like me, only he's unlucky and lives in the Land of Bad Luck— most of the time."

Uh-oh, I think. "What do you mean by '*most* of the time'?"

Posey swallows hard. "Sometimes imaginary opposites can come to the Real World. Those are called Bad Luck Days."

I look toward the girls' room because now I know I probably just met Posey's opposite.

"But how did he get here?" I ask.

Posey's eyes widen, and he gasps. "He must have come through a *broken mirror*, like the one I broke in your . . ."

But before Posey can finish, the floor underneath me opens up and I tumble into darkness.

Chapter Seven

The Land of Bad Luck

By now I am used to falling through holes in the floor, but I will never get used to the landing.

I hit the ground with a thud. Wherever I am, it's raining. Then I look up and discover it's only raining on *me*. I have my own personal rain cloud parked right over my head.

"Where am I?" I call out helplessly.

A bush rustles nearby. Something is trying to get out. I cover my eyes and peek through my fingers. It's Bathroom Mirror Posey! I know it's him because the leaf on his antler is on the opposite side of Posey's.

"Welcome to the Land of Bad Luck!" he says much too cheerfully.

I groan loudly. It feels like I've been in the Land of Bad Luck all day. *Obviously*.

"My name is Yesop," Bathroom Mirror Posey says. "And I'm *so* happy you're here to celebrate Bad Luck Day!"

I wipe raindrops off my face with the back of my hand.

"Well, I'm Daisy," I respond. "And would you please make it *stop* raining on me?"

Yesop's mouth drops open. "Why would you want it to stop raining?" he asks in surprise. "Personal rain clouds are only for our most honored guests. We don't even charge extra for wet, stringy hair, soggy clothes, and general misery!"

I blow a raindrop off the end of my nose. "Well, may I at least have an umbrella?"

Yesop playfully swats me. "You are such a silly!" he says. "In the Land of Bad Luck we only open umbrellas when we're *inside*. It's much worse luck!"

I slowly nod because now I'm beginning to understand. Unlucky things are *normal* in the Land of Bad Luck.

"Would you like me to show you around?" Yesop asks.

I stand up and wring out my shirt, which is kind of pointless because it's still raining.

"Sure, why not?" I say with a sigh. "I've had rotten luck all day, so what's a little more bad luck?"

Yesop grabs me by the hand and takes off running. My personal rain cloud and I do our best to keep up.

We run all the way to the edge of a beautiful pond. It has a sandy beach and a float with a curvy slide.

"Doesn't this look inviting?" Yesop asks. I have to agree, it looks *very* inviting. I want to slip down that slide right now.

"Well, fortunately, it's not what it looks like!" Yesop happily goes on. "The water is *freezing*, the sand is full of pesky fleas, and the slide feels like sandpaper all the way down! Isn't that *marvelous*?"

I shake my head in wonder. "Well, that's just *marvy-doo!*" I say, because honestly, I'm not sure what else to say. But I definitely don't go for a swim.

The next stop on our tour is a pizza shop. I breathe in the yummy smell of baking bread, melting cheese, and oregano. *Mmm,* I say to myself.

Yesop shoves a pizza paddle into the oven and pulls out a freshly baked pizza. I rub my hands together.

"Do you like fresh, hot pizza?" Yesop asks.

I nod wildly. Of course I do! *Obviously.*

"Then you're going to love *this* pizza! The cheese is scorching hot and ready to burn the roof of your mouth. If you don't drop your slice on the ground from the heat, then you'll pull off all the toppings with one bite. Isn't that perfectly *awful?*"

My shoulders slump.

"That is a fine example of perfect awfulness," I agree, and it's no surprise I pass on the pizza.

Then Yesop and I go to the movies.
"Are the movies here all about bad
luck?" I ask.

Yesop waves me off. "No, of course not!" he says. "The bad luck is only for the moviegoers!"

Well, that should've been obvious, I think.

Sure enough, the theater is all out of popcorn. *Ugh.* And we're so late,

we've already missed the previews for upcoming movies. *Grr.* And then we have to find seats in the dark. Then we can't find two seats together, so we give up and leave.

"Wasn't that the worst?" Yesop asks.

I nod, and my teeth are chatter-
ing like crazy because did I mention
the air-conditioning at the movies was
colder than the North Pole?

Yesop laughs and holds up one
finger. "Oh, I have one more place to

share with you!" he tells me. "And it's the most magical place in the entire Land of Bad Luck!"

Well, that can't be good, I think. I am sure Yesop saved the worst for last.

CHAPTER EIGHT

Under the Rainbow

I was right. So. Very. Right.

Our next stop is the Stinky Forest! And it lives up to its name!

"Do you know why it's so stinky?" Yesop asks as he takes a deep breath of the foul air. "It is full of rotten cheese, old moldy socks, and *skunks* that spray for *fun!*"

I can't help it. I begin to back away.

"*Please!*" I beg. "No more of your five-star bad luck! I'm tired and very uncomfortable."

Yesop's face falls. "Oh dear, have you had too much of a bad thing?"

I nod wearily.

"I understand," Yesop says. "Let's rest on this slimy rock that's covered with ants."

I sit down because who cares? I'm soaking wet already. And no sooner do I get settled than something catches my eye. It's Posey! The *real* Posey. He's peeking out from behind a tree and trying to tell me something.

He puts a finger to his lips, which I know means *Don't say anything*. Now he's pointing at something on the ground in front of me.

I look down and notice a shiny penny at my feet. I pick it up.

Yesop notices it too.

"Is that a . . . lucky penny?" he asks.

I hold the penny so he can see it, and Yesop gasps. At the same time, the sun comes out—even on *me*! And there's a *rainbow*!

The sun makes Yesop yowl, and he covers his eyes with both hands. He's not used to bright lights.

Then Posey rushes in and grabs my hand. "Quick!" he whispers. "We have to run under that rainbow."

So I keep running because I really want to leave the Land of Bad Luck. *Obviously*. But I also feel bad about ditching Yesop without saying good-bye.

Then we zip right under the rainbow.

ZING!

I get up and stumble behind Posey,
clutching the lucky penny in my fr
hand.

"But what about Yesop?" I as
Posey keeps running. "We v
about him later!" he says.

The next thing I know, we're back in the hallway outside my classroom. I pat my hair and my clothes. Everything's dry, and even my shirt is clean!

"That was *close!*" Posey says. "You had better hang on to that lucky penny. It will keep Yesop from bothering you."

I look at my lucky penny. I'm happy to have it, but I still wished I could've said good-bye to Yesop.

☆ Chapter Nine ☆

The Art Show

Nobody has noticed I was gone—that's because no time has passed while I was in the Land of Bad Luck. *Whew!* The rest of my school day is neither lucky *nor* unlucky, which is *okay* by me.

But one thing bothers me: *Was it really just bad luck that brought Yesop and me together, or was there something more to it?*

Soon the end-of-the-day bell rings. Today we get out of school early to go to the art show. Jasmine and Lily left early to finish setting up.

Mr. Roberts whistles to get our attention. "Time to make a line!" he announces.

Chairs scrape across the floor as we hop from our seats to line up. Then the class shuffles down the hall to the gym with the rest of the school. We pass under an archway of colorful coffee filters. The coffee filters have been decorated to look like spring flowers. It's truly magical!

The inside of the gym looks like a *real* art gallery! The walls are covered with masterpieces from every grade. The portrait gallery is called The Faces of Weaverley Elementary. I spy my own self-portrait hanging on the wall! I like how it feels to be a true artist. Then I admire my classmates' art.

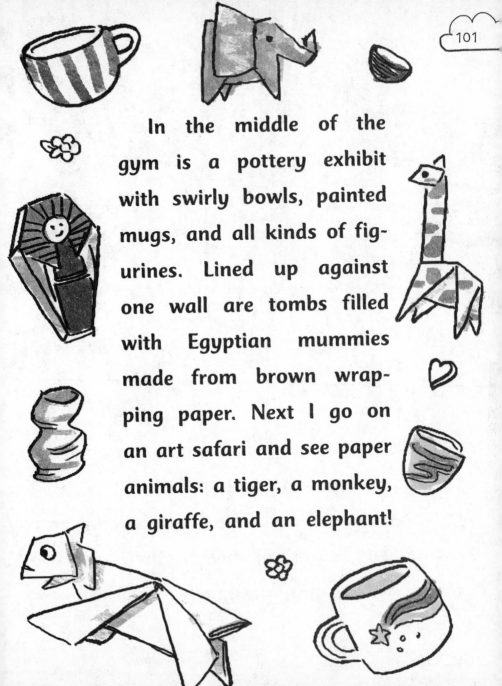

In the middle of the gym is a pottery exhibit with swirly bowls, painted mugs, and all kinds of figurines. Lined up against one wall are tombs filled with Egyptian mummies made from brown wrapping paper. Next I go on an art safari and see paper animals: a tiger, a monkey, a giraffe, and an elephant!

There's even a *giant* paper dragon hanging from the ceiling!

As I round a corner, I spy Jasmine and Lily standing beside their art projects. Jasmine designed a beautiful

butterfly made of colorful tissue paper.
It's called *On Rainbow Wings*. Lily has
created a collage with tiny mirror tiles
and glitter. Her artwork is titled *Shiny
Dreams*.

"*Wow, I love your artwork!*" I tell my friends. I also tell them how much I love the whole gallery. We share a hug but not for long because Jasmine and Lily are going to be interviewed for the school *newsletter*.

After they leave, I take time to really admire my friends' art. Then I notice my face reflected in one of the tiny mirrors on Lily's artwork . . . only it's not *my* face! It's Yesop's! I step closer and notice something else. Yesop's face looks very sad.

"Yesop!" I whisper. "Are you okay?"

Yesop looks away.

"Please don't be sad," I say. "I'm *so* happy to see *you*! And I'm really sorry I didn't get a chance to say thank you or good-bye."

Yesop looks at me now, so I keep going.

"I wish I could give you a hug for sharing the Land of Bad Luck with me!" And it's true, even if I *didn't* have fun—it *was* an interesting adventure.

Well, before you can even say "broken mirror," Yesop bursts out of an itty-bitty mirror and gives me a *great huge* hug. The hug happens so fast, we both lose our balance and bump right into the wall.

"Oh no, Daisy!" I say, because I also always say "Oh no, Daisy" whenever I knock something over. *Obviously.*

Jasmine's and Lily's art projects fall onto the floor. I try to catch them, but the two pieces land propped up against each other. Now Jasmine's butterfly looks like it's seeing itself in Lily's collage—and the lights shining from above create a colorful burst that reflects all around the gym!

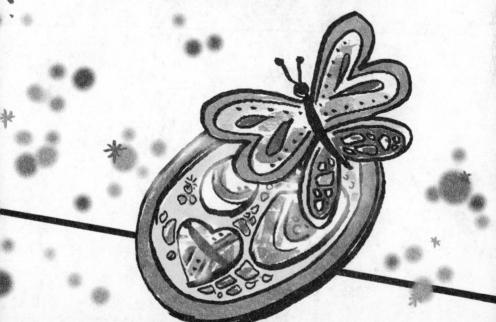

"How pretty!" I cry. "These work even better *together!*"

Yesop admires the new art too.

"See?" he says, looking at me. "Sometimes a little bad luck can lead to something *beautiful!*"

A warm, happy feeling washes over me.

"*Lucky* us," I say.

Then we share a smile. And this time, when we say good-bye, it's *perfect*.

Chapter Ten

A Blue-Ribbon Day

Lily and Jasmine come back and see what's happened. Jasmine covers her mouth with her hand. Lily gasps. I shift my feet uncomfortably.

Do they like what they see? Or are they mad at me? I look from one friend to the other and back again. Then a smile spreads across Jasmine's face.

"I love it," she says.

Lily grins too. "Same here," she agrees. "I just wish *we'd* thought of it."

I feel my shoulders relax, and I breathe a sigh of relief. I put one arm around each of my besties. Then our teacher, Mr. Roberts, comes over with a black zippered case in his hand. He stops and studies the fallen artwork.

"Stunning," he says. Then he unzips his black leather case, and I can't help myself. I peek right inside. The case is full of colorful satin ribbons—blue, red, yellow, and white. Mr. Roberts pulls out a blue ribbon.

"This is a dazzling *first-place* display!" he declares.

Jasmine, Lily, and I pose for a picture.

"This is all thanks to you, Daisy!" Jasmine says.

"Yeah, you are our good luck charm," adds Lily. "Without you, our art could've fallen on the floor and been ruined!"

Then I share what I learned from Yesop. "Sometimes a little bad luck can lead to something *beautiful*!"

As soon as I say it, I hear some familiar giggles. I look over at the window, and there in the reflection I see Posey *and* Yesop waving. I sneak a little wave back at my imaginary friends.

Then I wipe my brow because it's been quite a day! And I'm so thankful everything's back to normal. *Well, at least as normal as it can be for me, Daisy Dreamer!*

"I spy with my little eye . . . a fairy!" Luna exclaimed.

"A fairy?" Itty giggled. "Good one, Luna! We are more than a hop, skip, and a jump from Fairy Forest. There are no fairies in this field!"

"She's right, Itty!"

Itty turned to the sparkling flower that had just spoken.

"Really?" Now Itty believed it. Flowers rarely spoke. When they did, it was because they had something very important to say.

Look for more Daisy Dreamer books at your favorite store!